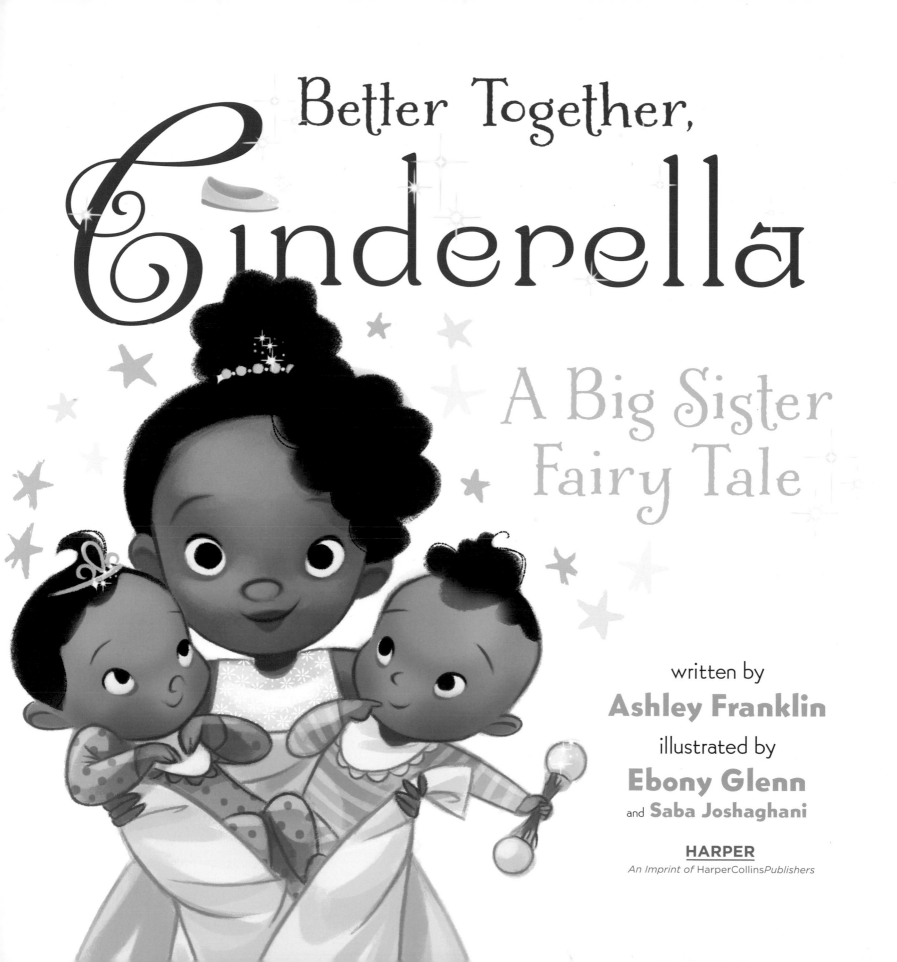

Better Together, Cinderella

A Big Sister Fairy Tale

written by
Ashley Franklin

illustrated by
Ebony Glenn
and **Saba Joshaghani**

HARPER
An Imprint of HarperCollinsPublishers

ISBN 978-0-06-302954-5

The artist used Adobe Photoshop to create the digital illustrations for this book.
Typography by Jeanne Hogle
21 22 23 24 25 RTLO 10 9 8 7 6 5 4 3 2 1

First Edition

To families: the ones we're born into
and the ones we've pieced together.
—Ashley

Once upon a time, Tameika got big news that would change everything. She would soon play her most important role—that of a big sister.

Tameika asked her best friend, Khadija, for advice. "How will I know what big sisters do?!"

"Practice, practice, practice!"

"Just pretend it's a role for one of your auditions."

Tameika was nervous, but jittery legs and a fluttery tummy had never stopped her from shining onstage. And nothing was going to stop her from shining as a big sister, either.

Tameika did her research.

She dressed for the part.

And she rehearsed.

Tameika was super excited to meet the twins, but when they arrived, big sister bliss was replaced by big sister blues.

Things at home were different.

Now there were more baby bottles than backyard ballets,

more laundry mountains
than bubble mountains,

and more dirty
diapers than daddy
kisses.

Even lullabies and puppet shows were
thanklessly met with tears and slobber.

TAMEIKA'S
PUPPET
THEATER

"Maybe Sophia and Asher don't like me," Tameika told her parents.
"Nonsense!" said Mom.
"You just have to be patient," said Dad.

Tameika tried teaching Sophia and Asher all the things she loved, but they were always too much of all the wrong stuff—gassy, wiggly, or fussy—to pay attention. Tameika wished for a big sister script so she'd know what to do.

Tameika didn't get her wish, but she did get news of something even better. The new mayor was throwing the first-ever community family ball. It promised to be a magically fun time where families could dress up and dance the night away. There would be a prize for the family with the best entrance.

This gave Tameika a grand idea.

"No one in the history of ever made a better entrance than Cinderella!" she told Khadija. "I'll make it a perfect night for the twins, and that'll show them I'm a good big sister."

To put her plan into motion, Tameika called in an expert. From the sharpness of his lineup to the crispness of his sneakers, Uncle Derrick was the best dresser Tameika knew.

On the night of the ball, he did not disappoint.

Tameika was ready to go, but her parents were taking forever to get the twins ready.

"Go ahead, princess. We'll meet you there," said Dad.

The ball was off to a magical start when she and Uncle Derrick arrived. Tameika smiled as she watched some of the other entrances. But as time went on, she worried when the rest of her family still wasn't there.

Things were definitely different.
Maybe there was one parent for Asher, one for Sophia . . .

"And none for me," Tameika spoke softly. She hugged Uncle Derrick tightly.

"Dry your eyes, Cinderella," he said.
"Your parents have never let you down.
They're not starting today."

Right on cue, Tameika saw her parents sprinting over with the strollers.
"Sorry we're late, princess." Dad kissed her forehead and Mom kissed her cheek.

It was their turn at last!

"It's our time to shine," Tameika said to Sophia and Asher in a singsong voice.

Tameika's grand entrance went perfectly . . .

until several loud POPs came from the balloon arch.

Startled, Sophia and Asher wailed. Tameika tried to continue, but all eyes were on the twins. This was a disaster. Tameika ran away.

Uncle Derrick followed and sat beside her in the carriage,
"You know, the perfect night sky isn't made up of one star
shining its brightest. Stars show their brilliance when they
shine together."

"I think this belongs to you."

Tameika thought about all the ways she'd tried to shine as a good big sister, yet there was something she hadn't tried: being herself.

Now was her chance.

Tameika curtsied to Asher

and placed her tiara on Sophia's head.

It wasn't a perfect night. But it was the perfect night to stop trying to be perfect and just have fun.

It was a magical beginning, indeed.

Everything *had* changed for Tameika, and she knew her new-sized family would live happily ever after.